Using this book

When going through this book
with your child, you can either read through
the story first, talking about it
and discussing the pictures,
or start with the sounds pages
at the beginning.

If you start at the front of the book,
read the words and point to the pictures.
Emphasise the **sound** of the letter.

Encourage your child to think
of the other words beginning with
and including the same sound.
The story gives you the opportunity
to point out these sounds.

After the story, slowly go through the
sounds pages at the end.

Always praise and encourage
as you go along. Keep your
reading sessions short and stop
if your child loses interest.

Throughout the series, the order in which the sounds
are introduced has been carefully planned to
help the important link between reading and writing.
This link has proved to be a powerful boost to
the development of both skills.

SOUNDS FEATURED IN THIS BOOK

j u y

The sounds introduced are repeated
and given emphasis in the practice books,
where the link between reading and writing is at the
root of the activities and games.

Ladybird books are widely available, but in case of
difficulty may be ordered by post or telephone from:

Ladybird Books – Cash Sales Department
Littlegate Road Paignton Devon TQ3 3BE
Telephone 01803 554761

A catalogue record for this book is available
from the British Library

Published by Ladybird Books Ltd Loughborough Leicestershire UK
Ladybird Books Inc Auburn Maine 04210 USA

Ladybird

Say the Sounds
Dinosaur
rescue

by JILL CORBY
illustrated by ANN JOHNS

Jj

jam

jelly

juice

jump

June

Jenny

4

just

jog

jaws

jug

judo

job

Jasmin

juggler

5

Uu

umbrella

up

under

us

Unwin

ugly

uncover

udder

underground

understand

undress

uncle

umpire

7

Yy

Say the sound.

yellow

you

Yorick

young

yes

8

yacht

yard

yam

yak

year

The children were all hard at work. Mrs Green was going over their work on dinosaurs with them.

"I like this dinosaur work,"
Jenny said to her friend Jasmin.
"And no one knows just why they
disappeared," Jasmin told her.

"I should like to see a dinosaur
now," Ben said to his friend
Unwin.
"Why do you think they all
disappeared?" Unwin asked them.

"You can stop now, children, and go out to play," Mrs Green told them.
So the children all ran out to play. Mrs Green went to have some tea.

"I should like to play hide and seek," said Jasmin.

"Yes. Let's play hide and seek," Jenny said.

"Why can't we play? We should like to play hide and seek, too," Ben and his friend Unwin said.

"Who will count?" asked Jenny.
"You can count first," Ben said
to her.
So Jenny ran to the big tree
to count. "I will count here,"
she told them.
When Jenny looked, they had
gone.

She saw Jasmin first.
Then they ran to look for the
boys. Jasmin knew that the
boys had climbed into the pipe.

But when they went to look,
the boys were not there.

The girls knew that Unwin and Ben had climbed into the pipe to hide.
When the boys were in the pipe, they could see something strange at the other end. When they had climbed out of the other end, they were in a strange land.

It was very hot.
"Why is it so hot here?" Ben
asked Unwin.
"I don't know, but it's a very
strange land," Unwin said.

As the two boys went to look at the trees, they saw some huge footprints.

"What creature made a footprint as big as this?" asked Unwin.

"I don't know, but it must be a huge creature," Ben told him.

"Where do the footprints go?"
asked Unwin.
So they followed the footprints
over the sand. They walked by
the footprints and followed
them over the hill.

Then they saw the dinosaur.
He was huge and he looked
very hot. He looked strange.
He was not like the
dinosaurs in their
work for
Mrs Green.

Then he roared at them. The
boys were scared so they
climbed up a tree to hide.
They had to get very high. The
dinosaur roared and roared as
he looked at them.

Jasmin and Jenny climbed into
the pipe to look for the boys.
They saw the strange land at
the other end.
The two girls climbed down out
of the pipe. They followed the
huge footprints and then they
saw the dinosaur by the tree.

The two boys shouted to them from the tree.

"Help! Help! Get some help. He is going to eat us."

As the dinosaur roared, the girls could see his teeth. They knew that he was not dangerous. He would not eat them.

The girls looked at the boys and laughed and laughed. They knew that the boys were not pleased with them. "That dinosaur is not dangerous," Jasmin laughed.
"He's going to eat us. How do you know he's not dangerous?" shouted Ben.

"How can you know?" shouted Unwin.

"Look at his footprints," Jenny told them. "He has no sharp claws, no sharp claws at all."

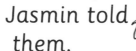

"He will not eat you. He is a vegetarian. A dangerous dinosaur has sharp claws and sharp teeth," Jasmin told them.

The girls went up to the dinosaur to talk to him. They were surprised that he could talk. He told them that he was a vegetarian.
The boys climbed down out of the tree and looked at his teeth and claws.

They could see that the dinosaur had no sharp teeth and claws. He had to be a vegetarian. He told them that his name was Yorick. He looked very sad.

"You see, there are no other dinosaurs left," he said, sadly.

"I am the only one of us left. All the others have gone," Yorick told them, sadly.

"But why have they all gone?" asked Ben.

"It's too hot for us now, so I am the only one left," said Yorick.

They went with Yorick to look at his cave. It was not so hot in the cave.
"I have to stay in the cave when it gets too hot," he said to them.
"I only go out when it's not so hot."

Yorick told them that there was
no one left to talk to and play
with. He asked the children to
play with him.
They all rode on his back. They
went up and down the sand hills.
They laughed and laughed.

It got hotter and hotter.
"I am going back to my cave now," Yorick said. "It's just too hot for me out here."
He walked sadly back to his cave.

As it got hotter and hotter,
Unwin had an idea.
"Shall we take Yorick back with
us?" he asked. "Shall we take
him back to see Mrs Green and
the other children?"

"But how shall we get him into
our pipe?" asked Jasmin.
Then Ben had an idea.
"Can he make himself very long
and thin?" he asked. "Then I
think he will fit in."

Yorick was so pleased that he
made himself very long and
thin. Then the children took him
to the pipe.
"Do you think he is long enough
and thin enough to fit into our
pipe now?" asked Jasmin.

Yorick squeezed himself into the
pipe. He was just long enough
and thin enough to fit in.

Then Yorick squeezed and
squeezed himself out of
the pipe. He went with
the children to see
Mrs Green. She was
very surprised.
"This is our friend,
Yorick," they told
her.
"We knew you
would like to see
him," said Ben.

"He's going to stay with us now. He's the only dinosaur left," Jenny told her.

"What will your mum and dad say?" asked Mrs Green.

Point to the pictures which show words beginning with Jj.

How many did
you find?

Uu

Read these words.

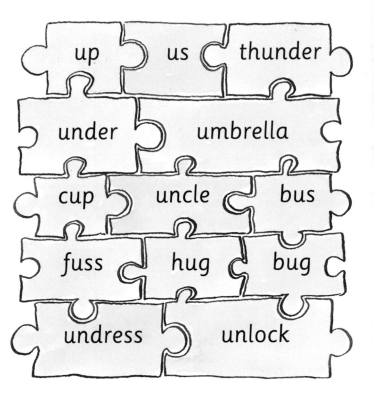

up us thunder

under umbrella

cup uncle bus

fuss hug bug

undress unlock

Can you think of more U words?

Yy

All these end with **y**.
Listen to the sound.

say	only
day	every
play	quickly
may	quietly
hay	lovely
they	hungry
tray	any
my	

New words used in the story

Page
Numbers

10/11   children work Mrs
dinosaur(s) friend
Jasmin just why
should Unwin

12/13   play ran went
hide seek

14/15   count boys knew
climbed pipe

16/17   girls other(s) end
land hot it's

18/19   as huge footprint(s)
followed

20/21   roared get(s)

42

Words introduced   58

Learn to read with Ladybird

Read with me

A scheme of 16 graded books which uses a look-say approach to introduce beginner readers to the first 300 most frequently used words in the English language (Key Words). Children learn whole words and, with practice and repetition, build up a reading vocabulary.

Support material: Pre-reader, Practice and Play Books, Book and Cassette Packs, Picture Dictionary, Picture Word Cards

Say the Sounds

A phonically based, graded reading scheme of 8 titles. It teaches children the sounds of individual letters and letter combinations, enabling them to feel confident in approaching Key Words.

Support material:
Practice Books, Double Cassette Pack, Flash Cards

Read it yourself

A graded series of 24 books to help children to learn new words in the context of a familiar story. These readers follow on from the pre-reading series, **Read together**, and can be used in conjunction with any Ladybird reading scheme.